MOVE MOUNTAIN

With thanks to Alison Stewart
and Lucy Murphy
www.hopeworksproject.com

For our dear friend Connie, who has moved her
own mountain – with incredible strength and grace.
C. A.

For my family.
G. M.

OXFORD
UNIVERSITY PRESS

Great Clarendon Street, Oxford OX2 6DP

Oxford University Press is a department of the University of Oxford.
It furthers the University's objective of excellence in research, scholarship,
and education by publishing worldwide. Oxford is a registered trade mark of
Oxford University Press in the UK and in certain other countries

Text © Corrinne Averiss 2022
Illustration © Greg McLeod 2022

The moral rights of the author and artist have been asserted

Database right Oxford University Press (maker)

First published 2022

British Library Cataloguing in Publication Data available

ISBN: 978-0-19-277866-6

1 3 5 7 9 10 8 6 4 2

Printed in China

Paper used in the production of this book is a natural,
recyclable product made from wood grown in sustainable forests.
The manufacturing process conforms to the environmental
regulations of the country of origin

MOVE MOUNTAIN

CORRINNE AVERISS

OXFORD
UNIVERSITY PRESS

GREG McLEOD

Mountain had never seen the sun rise.

Each morning,
the sun's rays sent colour
and brilliance to the hills
around him.

But **his** face remained shaded and cool.
The sun always rose behind his rocky back.

'If I wasn't so heavy, I would
turn around,' he told Bird.

Bird was lucky, she could
go where she pleased.

So Bird went to Bear – who was strong – to ask if **he** could move Mountain.

Bear pushed with all his might.

One,

two,

but Mountain didn't
move one bit.

Bird said the sun floated
upwards gently.

Sometimes through clouds,
sometimes into endless blue.

And the whole world felt
warmer and brighter.

Mountain closed his eyes, he thought her
words sounded wonderful.

But when he opened them
again, he let out a heavy sigh –

'I just can't picture it ...!'

Bird wondered if music might help
Mountain to **imagine** the sunrise.
She asked Squirrel to play his Sunrise Song . . .

Mountain listened and smiled.
He loved it very much.
It sounded like the start of something,
it made him feel happy and alive.

But it only made him
wish more than ever
to see the sun rise.

Bird had one more idea!

That night, Mountain
received a special invitation.
It said, 'You are invited
to the sunrise.'

Mountain was so excited he hardly slept.

When dawn came, he looked across the valley
and wondered how this could be possible.
With eyes wide open, he waited . . .

Mountain asked Bird if she could describe the sunrise.

'We could move the sun instead?'
suggested Bear, excitedly.
Bird shook her head.
Bird knew about these things.

Suddenly!
A GIANT yellow balloon emerged
slowly and drifted up into the sky.

In a basket beneath ...

Bird led the flying chorus,

Squirrel played his song,

and Bear blew the balloon
upwards with all his might.

Mountain was moved.
He felt happy.
He felt alive.

He saw the kindness of his friends.

And just as Bird said . . .

the whole world felt
warmer and brighter.